BAREFOOT BEAR
PLAYS BALL

by Richard H. Eyster
Illustrated by Roberta Lee Collier

KALEIDOSCOPE

ISBN 0-8300-0337-1

Barefoot Bear Plays Ball
was prepared and produced by
Tern Enterprises, Inc.
Sagaponack Road
Bridgehampton, New York 11932

Cover and book design by Duncan S. McKenzie

Printed and bound in Hong Kong
by Leefung-Asco Printers Ltd.

Barefoot Bear™ is a trademark of
Tern Enterprises, Inc., Bridgehampton, New York

Produced exclusively for **Kaleidoscope**

Love and thanks to all of you:
Mom, Dad, Mary, Eliza, Rebecca, Sarah, and Jason

Yesterday was Barefoot Bear's birthday. His mother and father gave him a new blue sweat shirt with his name across the front, a fuzzy yellow hat, and a shiny harmonica.

But his favorite present was the brand-new baseball he got from his best friend, Marshall.

Early this morning, Marshall came over to call for
Barefoot. "Come on," Marshall said. "Let's go to the ball
field and have a game of catch."

But when they got to the field, some of the older kids were already playing. And the biggest one of all was pitching. His name was Grizz. Barefoot knew Grizz was a mean old bear.

"Can we play?" Marshall asked. Marshall was big for his age, and sometimes the older bears let him play with them.

"You can," Grizz said, pointing to Marshall. Marshall ran out onto the field.

Barefoot cleared his throat. "What about me?" he asked. "Can I play, too?"

"Not with us, peewee," growled Grizz. "You're too small."

Barefoot sat down on the grass and watched the game. But after a while, he was bored. This was no fun. "Marshall," he called. "I think I'm going home."

Marshall turned to Grizz. "Oh, why don't you let him play?"

Grizz was walking toward home plate. It was his turn to bat. He took a practice swing. "No," said Grizz. "He's too little."

Barefoot turned to his friend. "So long, Marshall," he said.

"Bye, Barefoot," Marshall said quietly. "See you later." Barefoot started for home.

Before he got very far, Barefoot heard a tremendous crack. He turned and saw the ball that Grizz had hit flying higher and higher. He wondered if he would ever be big enough to hit a ball that hard.

Suddenly, he heard everyone shouting his name. He stopped and looked back. They were shouting for him. They were shouting for Barefoot Bear.

Slowly, Barefoot turned and walked back to the ball field. "What do you want?" he asked.

"You can play with us," Grizz explained, ". . . *if* we can use your baseball." "Where's *your* ball?" asked Barefoot. "We lost it," said Marshall. "Grizz hit it too far." "Well, do you want to play or not?" asked Grizz.

"Why, sure," said Barefoot with a grin. "When do I get to bat?" "Later," said Grizz, as he grabbed Barefoot's ball. "Come on," he said to the others. "Now we can keep on playing."

"Whose team am I on?" asked Barefoot. "Not mine,"
said Grizz. "Go play in the outfield."

Barefoot ran to the outfield. "Here?" he called.
"Farther out," said Grizz.

Barefoot ran farther. "Here?" he called. "A little farther," shouted Grizz, with a laugh. Barefoot ran farther.

He was so far out that he could hardly see the other players. "That's perfect," yelled Grizz. "Now stay out there until we tell you to come in."

Barefoot stayed there for a long time. Nobody hit the ball to him. Nobody told him it was his turn to bat. He was so far out he could hardly see what was going on. After a while, he sat down and watched a ladybug crawling up a blade of grass, and he thought about the day when he would be big enough to hit the ball so hard . . .

Suddenly there was a tremendous roar. Barefoot
looked up. He was in a stadium full of people. They were
cheering and shouting something over and over.

Barefoot looked down. He was dressed in a pink-and-purple uniform that said "Boston Baked Bears," and he had a pink-and-purple cap on his head, and a million-dollar glove on his hand.

He looked up. And everywhere he looked, people were waving to him and cheering. All of a sudden, he realized they were shouting his name. They were all shouting "Bare-foot."

He looked around. Marshall stood on second base.
"Come on, Barefoot! It's your turn to bat. Hit a home run!"
Barefoot's team was behind by one run. If he could hit a

home run, he'd finally be . . . a hero. He looked up to see who was pitching. It was Grizz. Grizz could throw the ball faster than anyone. "Come on," Marshall called. "You can do it."

Barefoot walked over and picked up a bat. He wiggled his hat and wiggled his toes (as he always did just before he batted), then went over to home plate. He held up the bat, ready to swing. Grizz leaned back, and threw the ball as fast as he could.

It came at him so fast Barefoot could hardly see it.
He didn't even swing. "Strike one," said the umpire. The
pitcher grinned. Barefoot swallowed hard.

The pitcher leaned back and threw the ball again.
This one was even faster. Barefoot didn't swing. "Strike
two," said the umpire. Barefoot had only one more
chance to hit a home run. Or else his team would lose.

"You can do it, Barefoot," Marshall called to him. Up in the seats all around the stadium, the people were cheering louder and louder. "BARE-FOOT! BARE - FOOT!" Over and over they called his name. He couldn't let them down. He couldn't let Marshall down.

So he pushed his toes a little deeper into the dirt.
This time, he was going to do it.
The pitcher leaned back even farther than before.

The ball came flying—even faster than before. Barefoot swung the bat with all his might. There was a sound like thunder. He hit it!

The ball whizzed right past Grizz. "Yipes!" cried
Grizz. "What was that?" "Yahoo!" screamed Marshall, as
he started to run. "Come on, Barefoot!"

He'd have to make it to first base, second base, third base, and all the way around to home plate to win the game for his team. But he knew he could do it.

He ran as fast as he could to first base. As he ran to second, he tipped his hat to the cheering crowd. By the time he got to third base, he was almost skipping with joy.

But as he started toward home, Marshall suddenly cried, "Look out, Barefoot!" There, right in front of him, stood Grizz. Grizz had the baseball. If he tagged Barefoot with the ball, the game would be over. Barefoot's team would lose.

But Barefoot wasn't worried. He remembered what Marshall had said. "You can do it, Barefoot." And he could.

Barefoot started running as fast as he could—right at Grizz.

Just when it looked as if Grizz would tag him, Barefoot curled himself up into a tiny, little ball and rolled
right between Grizz's legs.

"Hey!" Grizz cried out.

But Barefoot was already standing on home plate. He had won the game. "Sometimes it's better to be small," he said to Grizz. Marshall ran toward him. His team ran toward him. They lifted him onto their shoulders and called out his name. Barefoot was a hero.

Over and over they tossed him in the air. Over and over they shouted his name. And over and over, someone was tugging at his sleeve. Barefoot Bear looked around. It was Marshall, his old friend, Marshall.

Barefoot looked up. There wasn't any stadium.

He looked down. He wasn't wearing a uniform. He was wearing his regular old clothes. He hadn't hit a home run. He wasn't really a hero. It was all just a daydream. He was plain old Barefoot Bear.

"Are you okay, Barefoot?" Marshall asked. "Oh, yes, I'm all right, I guess," said Barefoot.

Barefoot looked back at the ball field. "Where is everybody?" he asked.

"It's late, Barefoot. The game is over."

"Oh," said Barefoot. "I guess I never got a turn to bat."

"No," said Marshall. "No, I guess you didn't."

"Where did everyone else go?" asked Barefoot. "Oh, they went on down to the honey shop," said Marshall.

"Why didn't you go with them?" asked Barefoot. "They like you."

"Yes, I guess they do," said Marshall. "But then, I'm more their size."

"I'm still kind of little," said Barefoot. "Yes," said Marshall, "a little bit little."

"Here," said Marshall. "Here's your ball. Now that everyone's gone, we can play catch." Marshall tossed the ball. Barefoot reached out his glove. The ball hit his glove and fell out. But he didn't care. Barefoot knew he wasn't a baseball hero. Not yet, anyway.

But he liked his new baseball. And he liked to play catch. And he liked his friend, Marshall.

"Why didn't you go with them?" Barefoot asked again.

Marshall smiled. "I wanted to play catch with *you,* Barefoot."

"I'm not as good as the big guys," said Barefoot.

"No, that's true," said Marshall. "But you're more fun."

"I am?" said Barefoot with a smile. "Here, catch."
He threw the ball to Marshall as hard as he could. It went
right to him. "Nice throw!" said Marshall.

"Thank you," said Barefoot. "Thank you very much,
Marshall."